The Big Gift

Derek Fisher

DEDICATION

To my wife and daughter for providing me
the inspiration for this book as well as being
by my side through every adventure.

CONTENTS

Acknowledgments   i

Chapter One   1

Chapter Two   13

Chapter Three   19

Chapter Four   27

Chapter Five   36

Chapter Six   41

Chapter Seven   57

Chapter Eight   69

ACKNOWLEDGMENTS

Thank you to Kim Burger for providing superb editing and Heather Workman for bringing the characters in this book to life.

CHAPTER 1

Alicia's brown pig tails swayed in the wind as she was flying high on the swing alongside her friend, Cathy, who was kicking up some dirt with her shoes as she swung up and down. Cathy lived down the street from Alicia. The two had been friends for several years. Today was their last day of summer break and they wanted to get in all the swinging they could before the school year took away a lot of their free time.

"You are getting dirt all over those shoes," Alicia said with disgust, her scrunched up nose pushing up her glasses on her face.

"I got new ones for school." Cathy wiggled a little brown toe through a rip in the corner of her shoe. "Good thing too, these barely fit anymore." Although Cathy was taller than Alicia, her feet weren't that much bigger. Alicia wondered how she was still able to fit in her shoes from last school year but Cathy could not.

Cathy quickly looked over to Alicia. "Your birthday is in a few weeks, right?"

"Yes!" Alicia was grinning ear to ear. "My mom told me I'm having my party at the new indoor bounce place."

"What do you think you are getting for your birthday?" Cathy knew she was asking the big question.

Alicia started to swing slower as she thought. She had lots of interests so it was hard for her to pick something. Some weekends she would beg her mom to take her to the craft store and get some supplies for a project. Other times she would just grab some leftover boxes to make a cat house for Sprinkles, her older cat. Sprinkles really did not care too much for the attention, but really appreciated the boxes. She also liked slime. Making slime, playing with slime, playing with her friend's slime—it really didn't matter because it was fun to do and make. What kid didn't like playing with slime? Board games and cards games were always a big hit in her house as well. On family game night, her parents would break out the board games and they would pass a few hours playing together.

There was one thing she was really hoping for on this birthday. She had a good feeling this year was finally the year she would get one—a tablet.

Most of her friends had a tablet or even a phone. Alicia had been preparing her parents for months by giving them hints. She would tell her mom that finding new slime recipes would be easier with a tablet. If only she had one instead of having to borrow her mom's phone or her dad's old tablet. Even better, Alicia would suggest that a tablet would help her with her homework. That idea was sure to help convince her parents!

She had also tried to be especially good this year. She kept her room clean and she would even help with extra chores around the house—sometimes without being asked! And her parents took notice. Alicia was hoping all the hints and showing how she was responsible would help her finally get a tablet.

One day, when her dad asked her what she wanted for her birthday, she finally came right out and said, "A tablet."

To her surprise, her dad said, "Possibly."

Alicia was suddenly reminded that Cathy had asked her a question. Cathy had stopped swinging and was just looking at Alicia who had already stopped swinging while she was thinking.

"Well?" Cathy rolled her eyes, showing her impatience.

"Books and a slime kit, I guess." Alicia looked down and dug her feet into the dirt to give herself a push on the swing. She didn't want to be disappointed, just in case she did not get the tablet.

"Bah, that's boring!" Cathy started to swing with Alicia again. As they passed each other going back and forth, she exclaimed, "Maybe you'll get a tablet!"

"Possibly." Alicia smiled, thinking about what her dad said.

The girls spent every bit of daylight left in the day outside. Both were sad the summer break was ending, but they were also a little excited to see some of their friends again and get into a new school year. As the sun set, Cathy's mom yelled for her to get home so the girls said goodbye, knowing they would see each other the next day.

Alicia went home and packed her school bag with supplies for the next day. Her dad had her favorite dinner, chicken tacos, waiting as a treat for making it to a new school year. She watched some television after dinner and then started getting ready for bed. The evening was going by quickly and Alicia was beginning to feel some of the excitement for the next day.

She didn't have to wait long. The next morning came quickly when Alicia was greeted by a knock on her door. "Rise and shine, sleepy head," her dad said as he cracked the door open a little bit. "It's the first day of school! You don't want to miss the bus."

Alicia forgot how hard it was getting ready for school. She was not a morning person! It was not too long before her dad called into her room again to ask if she was out of bed yet. She slowly rolled out of bed with a groan. Walking over to her closet, she took out a new outfit her mom bought her and got dressed. Then she walked into the bathroom to brush her teeth and her hair. The thought of a new school year and seeing her friends was helping to motivate her.

She ran to the kitchen to get her breakfast. In her house, mornings were typically very rushed as everyone was getting themselves ready for either work or school. Alicia ate a bowl of cereal while watching her parents hustled between the kitchen, living room, and bedroom as they got themselves ready.

As her mom threw a few extra snack items into Alicia's lunchbox, she told Alicia she only had a few more minutes to get to the bus stop. Alicia quickly finished the rest of her breakfast, put the bowl in the sink, and grabbed her bag.

"Wait!" her mom exclaimed, grabbing her camera. "We need a picture from the first day of school."

Her dad ran over to Alicia and fixed her collar on her shirt and pushed back some stray hairs. Her mom began taking pictures of Alicia every few steps and asking her to go to one side of the sidewalk and then the other side because the lighting was better. Her parents were obviously more excited about the first day of school than Alicia. Finally breaking free of the pictures, Alicia walked to the bus stop ahead of her parents.

The other neighborhood kids began to appear from different directions, each with their parents. Everyone was happy, taking pictures, and making comments about how big the children were getting. Alicia was relieved when the bus finally showed up because she didn't think she could pose for one more picture.

After greeting the bus driver, Mr. Wilson,

Cathy and Alicia walked down the aisle of the bus in search of the best seat for the new school year. It was a hard decision. They didn't want to be too close to the boys' section or too far in the back where the older kids sat. Alicia felt Cathy tap her shoulder and then point to an empty bench seat. It was the same seat from last year, and it was open. The two girls dove into "their" seat. The biggest question now was who was going to get to sit by the window. The friends agreed to switch seats on the ride home so Cathy could get the window then, but Alicia enjoyed sitting next to it now as the bus took off for another school year.

Along the way, the two friends began talking about what the new school year would be like. Cathy heard the new math teacher came from another school where they taught math differently. Alicia was good at math, but she was concerned about the new teacher and if he was mean. But soon the girls were laughing when Cathy reminded Alicia about the time Jackson ate a banana in the cafeteria and started to run around making monkey sounds. The lunch lady, who everyone thought was very nasty, was not happy with Jackson. She told him to sit down at a table by himself for the rest of lunch time. The monkey business was over for Jackson that day.

While Alicia was laughing, she looked out the window and saw the school building getting closer. It still looked the way she remembered. Alicia could feel the butterflies in her belly. The first day was always exciting, but there was also some worry about how the school year would go, and what her teachers and classmates would be like. More importantly, she hoped the cafeteria finally got rid of those gross green beans they were always serving.

***

The bus pulled up to the school and the kids started to get off. There was a lot of activity in front of the school as kids were going in all directions. Some parents were helping their kids find where they were going and teachers were trying to direct other kids to the right classrooms.

Alicia and Cathy found their classroom when one of the teachers asked them which grade they were going into. "Room 204," the teacher said and then pointed down the hall.

Alicia was happy to see many smiling faces when she walked into her classroom. It was at least better than last year when one kid was crying for the entire day! Alicia saw some of her friends from last year in the corner by the coat hangers talking so she ran over to say hello.

The classroom was filling up with noise as all the kids were talking and wandering around exploring all the new sights in the room. Alicia could hear some of the kids telling stories about the places they went to on vacation with their family over the summer. She heard one boy telling a group of friends about the trip he took to the Grand Canyon.

"Yep, a big hole in the ground. As far as the eye could see." He stopped for a few seconds and was looking out past the group of kids as if he could still see the Grand Canyon. "You would think that after two days of driving, you'd get to see more than a hole in the ground."

A few desks down from Alicia was a loud group of boys talking about their summertime birthday parties. Alicia recognized the red-headed boy describing his brand-new birthday bike. It was Ben, who Alicia had known since kindergarten. He had grown a lot over the summer and was much taller than Alicia remembered. But he certainly still liked to talk. In fact, Ben loved to talk. And if he wasn't talking, he was moving. If he wasn't moving, he was talking. Alicia always thought it was funny that when Ben talked it looked like his freckles were dancing on his cheeks. Currently, Ben was describing every detail of his new bike to the group of boys. He told them everything from the color all the way to the pattern of the stickers he put on the bicycle's frame.

"Then next to the blue gorilla sticker, I put a yellow rocket sticker..."

As Alicia was trying to listen to Ben, she noticed over his shoulder, a shorter girl with black hair and blue eyes walking towards them. It was Megan. Although Alicia knew Megan for two years, she didn't spend much time with her. There was nothing wrong with Megan; she and Alicia were just different people. Likewise, Cathy was not a big fan of Megan. She would often say that Megan spent more time talking about herself than anything else. Even though Megan grew up in a similar neighborhood as Alicia, she sure wanted everyone to know she thought she was special.

"Hey, Alicia!" Megan said as she joined Alicia and Cathy.

"Hi, Megan." Alicia watched Ben run towards another group of kids on the other side of the room. She couldn't tell what was going on, but it looked like one of the boys was showing off a lunch box that had some sort of flashing lights on it. Alicia would definitely rather be over there than talking to Megan.

"Guess what I did this summer!" Megan didn't really wait for a response. "I went to sleepover camp, and I got a huge honking medal for running in a race!" She had a proud look on her face and put her hands on her hips like some superhero.

"Oh, that's cool," Cathy said, trying to seem interested.

"I took a lot of pictures of it. And I never took it off while I was at camp," Megan continued. "I'll bring it in to class someday. I bet nobody else got a medal this summer." She was clearly proud of this medal.

Megan always had to have the best and biggest of everything. Alicia even remembered the last lunch they had in the cafeteria at the end of the school year. Megan was bragging to everyone at the table about the size of the scoop of mashed potatoes she got. Everything seemed to be a competition with Megan. Alicia wondered whether Megan was really in competition with herself.

"My mom got me this new dress too for

the first day of school." Megan twirled around the girls, holding part of her dress in her hand so it seemed wider, like a princess dress.

"It's pretty." Alicia smiled at Megan and crossed her arms trying not to glance down at her own outfit to see if it was just as pretty. Cathy was a little less impressed as she just nodded.

The girls looked to the front of the class to find the teacher waving her hands and asking for all the students to get ready for class. "All right, everyone. Take your assigned seats. You'll find a label with your name on your desk." Before she could even finish the sentence, there was a burst of commotion as the students tried to get to their seats as fast as they could.

Alicia took her seat, waved to Cathy across the room, and looked to the front of the class. She was happy to begin a new year. She hoped the new teacher, new books, and new faces would bring some new surprises this year. Maybe even that tablet she'd been wanting.

CHAPTER 2

When Alicia's alarm went off, she pulled the covers up over her head, but that didn't stop the alarm. She waited a few more moments and then got out of bed to turn it off. As she walked to the bathroom to brush her teeth, she looked at her calendar on the wall and put an 'X' through today and then counted the days to her birthday. *Just two more weeks to go*, she thought. She figured she still had some time to convince her parents she was really looking forward to getting a tablet this year.

She finished getting ready for school and walked towards the kitchen. She could smell coffee and toasted waffles. She wasn't a big fan of coffee, but she did like toasted waffles.

She sat at the table as her dad walked into the kitchen with his shirt untucked and one shoe on. He took a seat next to Alicia to put on his other shoe. "So, Alicia, your birthday is in a few weeks. Any ideas about what you want?"

"I think I have enough clothes and books." Alicia didn't want to lead right into it. Instead, she watched her dad tie his shoelace and waited for his response.

"Maybe a pony then?" Her dad smiled as he tied the last loop of his lace. When he got up to put Alicia's waffles on a plate and pour himself a cup of coffee, Alicia gave her dad a look that said she would like a pony, but she knew he was only joking.

"I know you've been wanting a tablet, so your mom and I will talk about it." Her dad kissed her on the top of her head as he put her plate of waffles on the table. Then he grabbed his work bag and headed to the front door. "Have a good day. Go easy on the syrup!" he shouted back as the door closed behind him.

Alicia had a smile on her face as she poured the syrup on her waffles and took a bite. She felt a little better after hearing her dad mention the tablet. And she didn't even have to bring it up!

"The bus will be here in a little bit," her mom said as she came into the kitchen. "Finish up your breakfast and let's head to the bus stop." Her mom put a sandwich and some snacks into a lunch bag as Alicia gobbled up her last few bites of waffle and ran out of the door with her school bag half zipped.

Alicia found Cathy at the bus stop, but she couldn't contain the smile she had. "You look happy," Cathy said. Alicia just kept smiling as the bus came to a stop in front of them. "Well?" Cathy asked as they boarded the bus and made their way down the aisle.

Alicia couldn't stop thinking about what her dad said that morning and she just had to tell Cathy. "My dad said he's going to talk to my mom about getting me a tablet!" Alicia said happily.

"Wow!" Cathy was almost as excited as Alicia.

Getting a tablet meant Alicia would finally join the rest of her friends and classmates, many of whom already had one. Now when she overheard her friends talking about all the games and apps they played and used, she would understand what they were talking about. She at least knew enough to seem happy when her friends got very excited when they were talking about them.

During the whole ride to school, Cathy explained to Alicia all of the apps and games she should get first. Cathy was looking forward to having someone else to play with on a few games.

***

The school days began to run together as Alicia's birthday was approaching. Alicia was scratching off the days on her calendar and leaving hints about a tablet to her parents.

The morning before her birthday she sat in the kitchen eating breakfast with her mom. "Cathy said she uses an app on her tablet to help Ben with his math homework." Alicia looked up while chewing her cereal to see her mom's expression. Alicia was pretty sure giving her mom an example of a good use of a tablet would be a big help.

"Sounds like Cathy is being a good friend," her mom said, taking a bite of her toast.

Alicia smiled and finished up her breakfast. She ran to the bus stop with a little pep in her step and she took her normal seat with Cathy once they got on the bus.

"You look like you're having a good

morning." Cathy laughed.

"My birthday is tomorrow and I have a good feeling I'll be getting a tablet." Alicia smiled.

Ben suddenly jumped up from his seat behind Cathy and Alicia and leaned over the back of their seat. "You have to get TullyTown!"

"What is that?" Alicia gave Ben a puzzled look.

"It's like real life, only it's not real! You can work, build houses, buy some clothes, talk to people, and run around. You can even drive cars!" He stopped for a moment to think. "When I was playing last night, I drove a really fast car." He started to put both hands out in front of him as if he was driving. "But I ended up crashing into a bush. I saw a bunch of squirrels jump out and run away." As he said this, he flopped back into his seat. "I may have even scared a racoon," Ben said with a shrug.

Alicia and Cathy just looked at Ben. "Those poor squirrels," Cathy finally said to Ben.

"Anyway, make sure you get VideoMe," Cathy said as she turned back to Alicia. "It's an app to make your own videos." She looked over her shoulder. "You don't drive fast cars though."

"That's no fun," Ben huffed.

"I usually watch craft videos or people unboxing things," Cathy added.

"What do you mean by unboxing?" Alicia was confused. *Why would someone want to watch someone else opening something?*

"Noob." Alicia heard from across the aisle where Megan was sitting. In all the excitement of hearing about fast cars and squirrels, they didn't notice Megan got on the bus.

"What is a noob?" Alicia asked, unsure if she really wanted to know.

"A noob is a new person. Someone that doesn't know much." Megan explained like she did when she showed off one of her trophies or new clothes. "I'm not a noob because I have over five hundred friends on SocialBee." Alicia still seemed puzzled so Megan continued. "It's an app where you can text and send pictures to other people. It's called social media." Megan rolled her eyes.

Alicia was wondering how anybody could possibly know or keep track of five hundred people. "Do you know all five hundred of them?"

"I know them on SocialBee," Megan said.

Alicia didn't bother asking more question. In her head she started to count people who she would consider her friends and it was far less. She didn't think about that for long. She had bigger things on her mind. Her birthday was *tomorrow*! She just wanted to get through the day, get home, and go to bed. And everyone knows that no kid just wants to go to   bed!

CHAPTER 3

"Happy birthday, Alicia!"

Alicia's eyes slowly opened to see her mom and dad sitting on the end of her bed. As Alicia sat up, her parents gave her a big hug and began to sing an out-of-tune version of "Happy Birthday," which made Alicia's face turn red. But by the end of the song, all three of them were laughing. She finally made it to her birthday, and she was very excited.

Shortly after her parents left the room, Alicia smelled bacon and pancakes cooking. *Birthday breakfast!* She jumped out of bed and ran to the kitchen.

On the kitchen table was a stack of pancakes—her favorite breakfast food—and a few wrapped presents next to her plate. Her eyes moved from the presents to the pancakes and back again. She wasn't sure which one she was more excited for.

Alicia grabbed a plate and put a few pancakes on it. She could not help glancing at the presents on the table in between every bite. She tried to look right through the wrapping paper to see if she could see a tablet in one of box shaped presents.

Within a few bites, she finished the last pancake on her plate and rubbed her belly. "I think I might pop!"

"I hope not. That would be a big mess." Her dad looked at the pancake on his fork, sighed and put it in his mouth. Pancakes were not one of his favorite things to eat.

Alicia wanted to reach for one of the presents on the table, but she first looked to her parents to see if it was okay. "Go ahead," her mom said.

Alicia did a little dance in her seat while she picked up the first box and shook it lightly. There wasn't much sound in the box and it wasn't very heavy. She opened it up and dumped out a few pairs of socks and underwear. She groaned a bit as they spilled out on the table while her dad let out a little chuckle.

"Well, you do need them," Mom explained.

She picked up the next one on the stack and it was certainly not clothes. It was too heavy. Besides, how many pairs of socks and underwear could one girl have! When she opened the box, there were a few books and a gift card in it. She smiled and looked through the books.

"Thank you!" Alicia had already forgotten about the socks and underwear.

There was one last box on the table. She didn't bother shaking it since it was the last one. If there was any hope of getting a tablet, it was in this box.

She tore off the wrapping paper and lifted off the lid of the box. Alicia was greeted with a rectangular, shiny screen in the box. *A tablet!* All that practicing saying "thank you" before she went to sleep the night before was forgotten in her excitement and surprise.

Her dad smiled seeing Alicia's excitement. "I needed a new tablet and after your mom and I talked, we decided to give you my old one." Alicia was just staring at the tablet while holding it closely and looking at every corner of it. It was thin, shiny, and a bit heavy. It was a little worn and had a few scratches on it, but none of that mattered to her. She was happy she finally had her *own* tablet.

She finally took her eyes off the tablet and looked up at her parents who were both watching her. "Thank you!"

Alicia's dad picked up the tablet and asked, "Are you ready to get this party started? I spent some time last night setting it up for you, so let me show you a few things." Her dad showed her how to make a password only she and her parents would know in order to lock the tablet.

Alicia's mom leaned over as her dad was explaining the importance of a password. "Back when I was your age, I had a lock on my diary. My cousin Jody was always teasing me about trying to read my diary, so one birthday I asked for a diary with a key and lock."

Alicia thought having a password made her cooler, like she was a top-secret agent.

"I put an app on here so your mom and I can see how you're using it," Dad said as he tapped on the screen a few times. "We want to make sure you stay safe while using the tablet. There are a lot of crazy people you might run into using this thing," her dad warned.

Alicia told her dad about some of the other apps her friends were using, like TullyTown, SocialBee, and VideoMe. It took some time for her father to examine the apps before he installed them on the tablet.

"So, Alicia, let's say you went to the store with me or Mom. If someone walked up to you and asked you to tell them your name and asked you other questions about yourself, would you tell them?" her dad asked.

"Is it someone I know?" Alicia looked at her dad.

"Nope, you have never seen this person before."

"I don't think so," Alicia said.

"Good. Think about that when you are playing some of these games and sending messages to people. You don't always know who you might be talking to," Dad explained. He looked back at the screen and tapped on a few other things. "Ask us if you have any questions or if something doesn't feel right, okay?" A few more taps on the screen and he handed over the tablet to Alicia. "Here you go." And in his superhero voice he added, "Remember, with great power comes great responsibility."

"Dad, it's just a tablet," Alicia said as her parents left the kitchen table.

Alicia held the tablet in her hands and was ready to enter a brand-new digital world. She saw the TullyTown app on the screen and decided to start there after all the things that she heard Ben talk about. She tapped the icon with her finger. The screen changed and showed a cartoon-looking town. Soon the screen changed again, and she saw what looked like a donut spinning and the words "loading" under it. Alicia felt like she was waiting for a long time as the donut kept spinning but the screen didn't change. Just as she was about to give up waiting, a different screen appeared that asked her to enter some information about herself so she could play.

"TullyTown is asking me to put in information to start playing," Alicia said to her mom who was sipping her coffee in the kitchen.

"What town?" her mom questioned as she put down her cup and walked over to Alicia.

"TullyTown. It's a fake town that you can do stuff in." Alicia handed the tablet over to her mom.

"Looks like you need to create an account to play." Her mom read the screen. "We need to create an ID for you. It's a way to identify you in the game, like a nickname in the game," her mom explained as she continued to enter in some information and tap on the screen. "But let's make sure it is something that doesn't give away too much information about you." Her mom thought for a few seconds. "How about your initials and a number, like aic25934?"

Alicia tried really hard to remember what her mom said. She understood the initials part, but not the numbers. Then she thought of a number that made more sense to her since it reminded her of a math game they played at school.

She finally said, "How about aic45901?"

"aic45901 sounds good to me." Her mom tapped on the screen a bit, read a few things, and then passed the tablet back to Alicia. "Any of your friends that you want to connect with will need your ID. So, do you think you can remember it?"

"Sure can! aic45901!" Alicia said proudly. It was more difficult to remember than "Alicia," but she was sure she would memorize it after a short time.

Her mom smiled. "Just remember, if you get a request from someone you don't know, I want you to talk to me or Dad. Not everyone that wants to connect with you is a friend and it's important that you are careful about who you talk to on this tablet." Her mom looked at the screen again and asked to see the tablet one more time. She tapped on the screen a few more times and handed it back to Alicia. "There. I also added some credit in TullyTown for you to use. Looks like you might be able to buy some things with it."

This was exciting news for Alicia. She wasn't sure what she could do with the credit yet, but knowing she could buy things in the game didn't sound too bad.

Her mom picked up her coffee again. "Just remember to have fun. These are games you are playing, and games are supposed to be fun. If you feel uncomfortable or have questions, let dad and me know."

"I will."

Alicia looked back at the screen and saw a little person standing in what looked like a store. The avatar just looked back at Alicia blinking its eyes. Alicia could make this avatar into anything she wanted. It was a way for her to create a little digital version of herself, and that was super exciting for her.

CHAPTER 4

Alicia looked at the little bald avatar on her screen. She had plenty of ideas about how she wanted it to look. She thought about making it look just like herself, or she could create something completely different.

As she tapped through all of the options on the screen for hair, eyes, skin, clothes, and accessories, she started to think more about her avatar looking like her.

Alicia got to work on her avatar. She started with brown hair and brown eyes, just like she had. Then she started to flip through the hair styles. Some were wacky, while others were plain. She ended up picking a style that she often liked to wear to school—pigtails with a bow on each side.

Alicia tapped on the screen a few more times to finish creating her face shape and details. She made some changes to the eyes and skin color and when she was satisfied, she moved on to pick her clothes.

She wanted a look that would stand out, so she made sure she looked at all of the options. She noticed some of the outfits had a little lock on them and they were colored gray, instead of being in full color like the rest of them. She figured it meant the clothes were not available for her to get. This wasn't a big deal since she found a shirt she could get. It was bright purple and had a big rainbow on it, which was perfect for her style.

Next, she found some shoes and shorts that matched. Well, not exactly. The shoes were as yellow as the sun, and the shorts were bright red. *No one will miss me in this outfit*, she thought to herself. Lastly, she was able to pick some accessories. So she finished her avatar's look with a fancy pair of glasses, but many of the other accessories needed credit so she took what she could get for free.

Alicia felt like her avatar was complete. This little version of her looked good and she was ready to get into TullyTown to see what it was all about. She saw a big button that said "Start" down at the bottom of her screen. She tapped the button on the screen and suddenly her avatar started falling from the bright blue sky down to the vivid green grass.

Landing softly on the grass, her avatar looked back at Alicia just blinking its eyes. It was a little overwhelming, as she wasn't sure what to do next. Large white birds were flying in the sky and the grass was swaying a little as the fake wind blew.

As she looked at her little avatar on the screen, a bubble appeared with arrows pointing to several areas on the screen. It was giving Alicia instructions on how to move around and use the different options in the town. This was a big help to Alicia and it did not take long for her to get the hang of moving the avatar. After only a few minutes, she was comfortable enough to start her adventure in TullyTown.

On the top of her screen was an arrow that pointed in the direction of the "Town Center." Alicia steered her avatar toward the town in the distance since she thought it was the best place for her to start. Using the directions the bubble gave her, she tapped on the screen a few times and her avatar started to move in the direction of TullyTown.

As she got closer, the green grass that she started on became buildings and streets. She stopped her avatar for a moment to look around to notice all the little things going on in the center of TullyTown. There were other avatars, cars, animals, trees, and plants. There were also a lot of buildings. Some were stores that sold animals, cars, furniture for the avatar's homes, as well as clothing and accessories for avatars. Some buildings looked like houses. Alicia was so focused on the game that when she heard her mom call her, she nearly jumped.

"Time to get ready for your birthday party," Alicia's mom called from upstairs.

Alicia looked up from the tablet. She nearly forgot she had a birthday party to go to. And best of all, it was hers!

She set the tablet down on the living room table and ran to her room to get ready for her party. She was looking forward to going to the new bounce place and was even more excited to be having her birthday party there. She got dressed and ready to go quicker than she ever had before.

***

As she climbed in the car with her mom, she began to tell her all about the avatar she created in TullyTown. Her mom seemed impressed by how quickly Alicia was able to get started on the game.

When they arrived at the bounce place, the manager greeted her mom. As they were talking, Alicia explored all the different slides, rides, and games. She wasn't exploring long before she glanced back towards her mom and saw Cathy walking in the front door.

Alicia couldn't wait to tell Cathy that she got a tablet for her birthday, so she ran as quickly as she could to the front. Cathy saw her coming and smiled wide as she saw Alicia's excitement.

"You'll never guess what I got for my birthday!" Alicia came to a stop in front of Cathy.

"Hmm... maybe a box of frozen broccoli?" Cathy asked. Alicia made the face you would expect someone to make when they hear the words "frozen broccoli". "I bet you got a tablet." Cathy said smiling.

Alicia nodded a little, and then a lot until her pigtails were bouncing up and down.

"Whoa! That's great!" Cathy started to bounce on her feet. "Did you get the VideoMe app?"

"Yes. My dad added it this morning, but I didn't try it yet," Alicia said.

"When you do get on there, you'll have to watch my video called 'Slime Three Ways.' It's three different slime recipes with three different colors," Cathy said proudly, but then she frowned. "Although, I dropped slime number two on the floor. My mom was *not* happy." Cathy put her hands on her hips when she said this but then shrugged.

"I only got a chance to play TullyTown today." Alicia noticed that Cathy looked a little disappointed. "But I will try VideoMe later tonight."

"I was watching a lady making squishy donuts that she was painting. She had some pretty good jokes, too." Cathy went on to tell Alicia all about the video she saw about a lady who made squeezable toys that she painted with a lot of different colors. While making these toys, the lady would tell jokes and talk to the toys using funny voices. It was obviously entertaining for Cathy, but Alicia was trying to understand why you would make a donut that you couldn't eat.

As Cathy was starting to explain other things the lady was making, some of their classmates were coming into the party. Each one said a quick "Happy birthday" while dropping off presents at a table and then they ran towards the first bounce slide they saw, even though their parents told them to remember their manners.

"Happy birthday, Alicia!" Alicia recognized that voice. Ben's mouth was open with awe as he looked around the place studying all the slides. "Whoa! This place looks awesome!" he said as he rocked back and forth on his toes. Ben didn't even notice that both Alicia and Cathy were now staring at him.

"Well, what are we waiting for?" Cathy started to turn towards one of the slides but stopped as she saw Megan walking through the entrance.

"Happy birthday, Alicia," Megan said.

"Thanks, Megan." Alicia was happy Megan was able to come to the party.

As Megan put the present down on the gift table she said, "Sorry, but it's not a tablet."

"That's okay, my parents actually got me one for my birthday!" Ben was even more excited as soon as he heard the news.

"Make sure you get on SocialBee," Megan demanded.

"I only played TullyTown so far." Ben seemed happy when he heard Alicia's response.

"Well, when you get SocialBee, send me a friend request. You'll get me closer to six hundred friends," Megan smiled.

"I thought you had five hundred friends?" Alicia looked a bit confused.

"That was a while ago," Megan said with a hurt look on her face.

"It must be hard to be friends with that many people. It would be a lot of work to know all of them." Alicia understood that Megan didn't really "know" all of these people, which made it odd that they were called "friends".

"It doesn't matter whether I know them or not. It only matters that I have a lot of people following me," Megan stated.

"What kind of tablet did you get?" Cathy was trying to change the subject.

Alicia turned back to Cathy. "My dad got a new one, so he gave me his old one."

"You mean it's used?" Megan made a disgusted face as she said this.

"What's wrong with that?" Alicia started to feel a little upset and embarrassed.

"Nothing, if you want to wait forever for your games to load."

Megan clearly couldn't understand how someone could live with an old tablet. The excitement Alicia had about getting the tablet and being able to be a part of what her other friends were doing was quickly disappearing.

"Well, if it was good enough for my dad, it'll be good enough for me," Alicia stated proudly.

"Don't listen to her, Alicia. Just make sure you get VideoMe when you get home," Cathy said. Alicia could always count on Cathy to cheer her up.

"And make sure you connect with me on TullyTown!" Ben was now rocking back and forth on his feet, still watching all the other kids playing in the bounce gym. "All right, I can't just stand here anymore and look at these beautiful bouncy slides!" With that, Ben ran to the nearest slide, leaving all three girls to catch up to him.

Each of the girls looked at each other and began to run after Ben, trying to beat him to the first slide. It was too late, by the time the girls got there, they could hear Ben laughing the entire way down to the bottom.

It will be a good birthday party, Alicia thought.

CHAPTER 5

After her birthday party, Alicia took a seat on the couch in her living room. Her belly was full of cake and her legs were tired from all the activity at the bounce place. She had the best birthday party ever and she was glad she got to see some of her friends. She was especially surprised by some of the presents she received. One of her friends got her a volcano kit that shot out slime! However, the look on her mom's face when she saw the volcano told Alicia her mom wasn't as excited about it.

As much fun as she had, Alicia was happy to finally be home. She was looking forward to being able to spend a little time with her presents. She opened some of the games she got and put them aside for family game night. She also left some of the toys about so she could sort them in her room later. As she was putting the gifts in different piles, she saw her tablet sitting on the table where she left it before leaving for the birthday party. Her mom was on the couch reading and her dad had the television remote in his hand with a football game on. Alicia decided she would try out another one of the apps on her tablet.

Picking it up, she unlocked it with her top-secret password. The screen was full of the apps her dad installed. Alicia tapped the VideoMe icon to watch some of the videos Cathy had mentioned. At Alicia's birthday party, while they were waiting for Cathy's mom to pick her up, Cathy told her about a video of a dog surfing at the beach and Alicia could not wait any longer to see that.

The app started to load and then Alicia saw a message that said she needed to create an account. *Another account?* Alicia thought to herself. She leaned over to ask her mom for help since her dad was getting either excited or upset over the football game, but Alicia could not tell the difference.

Her mom set down her book. "Well, do you think we should create a new ID, or would it be better to use the TullyTown one?"

"I don't want to have to remember too many things," Alicia replied.

"Let's keep things simple and use the same one then," her mom said as she began to tap on the screen. After a few more taps, her mom sat back and handed the tablet back to Alicia. "You're all set. Try to keep the videos to kids' ones. Remember, there are a lot of weirdos with cameras on the internet."

"Thanks, Mom, I will," Alicia said as she looked at the top of the screen and saw "aic45901" with a little outline of a person.

"Remember, like with TullyTown, if you don't feel comfortable about something just ask your dad or me." Both Alicia and her mom looked over at her dad who was off the couch and yelling something at the television. "Well, you can at least ask me," her mom said with a wink.

"I know."

Alicia looked back at the screen again. There were a lot of little pictures on the screen. Each was an image of a video as well as a place where she could search for more videos. She tapped on the search bar and typed in "surf dog" on the keyboard that appeared on the screen. The screen changed to show a list of images of dogs on surfboards. She picked the first one, and it did not disappoint. Alicia's mom even started to laugh as she peered over her book.

Alicia tapped on a few more videos. There were a lot of different things to see on VideoMe.

After the dog videos, she watched a cat wearing a tutu as it walked through someone's kitchen. She giggled as the cat took a few steps, looked up at its owner who was taking the video, and then laid down on the floor refusing to move. The cat was not excited about the outfit.

Alicia tapped on another video. This time it was a boy who was taking a video of himself eating jellybeans that were flavored with things that nobody should ever eat. He put one in his mouth, chewed for a few seconds, and then made a horrible face. "Eww! Vomit flavored!" He spit the jellybean out.

"Oh my," said Alicia with wide eyes.

She watched a few more videos of kids doing silly things, and some others of pets just being pets. She remembered that Cathy had told her she had some videos she made that she wanted Alicia to watch. But when she typed in "Cathy" in the search, a lot of videos came up. None of them were the Cathy she knew. She decided that searching wasn't going to work and she would have to ask Cathy tomorrow at school.

"Time to get ready for bed," she heard her dad say. He had already turned the football game off and was reading something on his phone. Apparently, time flies when you're watching videos of kids and animals. Alicia yawned and stretched, then bounced off the couch to get herself ready for bed.

Within a few minutes, she was in bed with a chapter book. After reading for a few minutes, her dad came in to say goodnight and turn off the light. She laid in bed looking at the ceiling where her glow-in-the-dark stars shined back at her. She couldn't help but think about the poor cat in the tutu that she saw on VideoMe. Alicia laughed to herself as she drifted off to sleep.

CHAPTER 6

Alicia woke up to her dad nagging her to get out of bed. Her alarm had gone off already, but Alicia got out of bed and turned it off before climbing right back under her covers. Except, then her dad used the "L" word while telling her to get out of bed.

"You're going to be late to school if you don't get out of bed and get ready!"

"Ugh! Ok, Dad. Sorry," Alicia moaned.

The morning was soon a flurry of activity as Alicia and her parents raced around to get ready for school and work. Alicia finished her breakfast and ran to the bus stop. As soon as she saw Cathy walking up the street to the bus stop, Alicia wanted to ask her about the video she made on VideoMe.

"I wanted to look up your video last night, but I wasn't sure where to find it," Alicia explained as Cathy set her bag down on the curb.

"You can friend me on VideoMe and see them on my page or you can look up the videos by my ID. It's QueenCathy2010."

Alicia thought that was awesome, or at least she thought it was way better than hers.

Cathy saw the look on Alicia's face and smiled. "It's my title, my name, and the year I was born," she said with her hands on her hips and her chin up. She was very proud of her ID.

"I should be able to remember that," Alicia said as the bus pulled up.

After both girls found their seats on the bus, Cathy asked, "Did you create an account on VideoMe?"

"Yeah, my mom helped me. My ID is aic45901." Alicia was a little embarrassed, especially after hearing Cathy's cool one.

"Oh my!" Ben leaned over the back of the seat. "I'll *never* remember that!"

"My mom thought it was best not to create a name that gives away too much information about me." Alicia looked down at her feet. She was feeling a little ashamed and she wasn't sure whether that comment would offend Cathy.

"Well, at least you don't have to worry about anyone else trying to use a similar one." Ben was looking for something nice to say. "Mine is 'ShellPanda'. You'd never know that it was me." He laughed.

"Oh, I'll definitely remember that one now!" Alicia started to laugh with Ben.

"Did you say yours was abc2345 or a2c9876?" Ben questioned, still trying to remember Alicia's ID.

"I know it is a little bit strange." Alicia grabbed a pencil and some paper from her school bag and wrote it down on slips of paper and gave one each to Cathy and Ben. "I'll look both of you up tonight when I get home. When you see a friend request come from a strange id, that'll be me."

Ben looked down at the paper scratching his head. He was still confused and still trying to make sense of what Alicia wrote. But there would be plenty of time for confusion later. The bus pulled up and it was time to get to class. The three got off the bus, made their way to their classroom, and dropped off their bags as the teacher called for them to take their seats.

"I'll talk to you later, Queen." Alicia

laughed and ran to her desk.

The day continued like most days. Math, spelling, lunch, recess, social studies, art, and then homeroom to wait to hear her bus had arrived.

Before she knew it, Alicia was home in no time. Alicia's mom greeted her at the bus stop and asked her to get an early jump on her homework, which brought an instant frown to Alicia's face. Still, she went to her bedroom, opened her school bag, and grabbed a few books and papers and then spread them out on her desk.

"I do not like social studies," Alicia said to herself as she picked up the first paper and read the instructions for what was due for tomorrow.

However, she figured she would get the hard stuff done first. She grabbed her pencil and began to work on the assignment. Within a few minutes, she glanced over at her tablet sitting on the corner of her desk. Her mind wandered as she thought about some of the videos she saw on VideoMe. She also thought about TullyTown. *I wonder if ShellPanda is in TullyTown right now*, she thought to herself. She almost laughed out loud at Ben's ID. *I wonder where Ben came up with that id!*

A few moments passed and Alicia realized she was just looking at her tablet and daydreaming. She shook her head and got back to her homework. She only had a few pages left anyway.

She finished working on the last page and closed the book with a thud. After organizing her papers and folders, she put it all back in her school bag. She zipped up her bag and picked up her tablet. Just as she sat back on the bed with her tablet, she heard her mom call from the kitchen asking her to help put the dishes away. Alicia groaned a little, but she set her tablet down. "Coming, Mom!"

Alicia ran to the kitchen and started to grab some plates and cups from the dishwasher and put them in the cabinet where they belonged. A few spoons and forks later, she looked at her mom.

"Do you have somewhere to be?" Her mom noticed Alicia was trying to hurry through the dishes.

"I was going to get on TullyTown and look for Ben," Alicia said.

Her mom smiled. "We have some time before dinner so have fun in TullyTown."

Alicia skipped to her room to grab the tablet and skipped back to the living room where she plopped herself down on the couch. She tapped the TullyTown icon and waited patiently for it to load. Finally, she was greeted by her avatar in all its bright colors in the middle of the town.

Before getting started, Alicia wanted to look up Ben. She found a spot on the screen where she could make a friend request. She tapped on the search button and typed in "ShellPanda." There were other names similar to ShellPanda with numbers or extra words at the end, but there was only one ShellPanda. Alicia clicked on that.

While she waited for Ben to respond, Alicia moved her avatar around the town. Like last time, TullyTown was full of activity. There were so many avatars going in all directions around the town as well as a lot of flashing lights and words around the screen as she moved. One little bubble popped up at the top her screen:

"ShellPanda accepted your connection request."

Alicia saw another button below the bubble that asked if she wanted to send a message to ShellPanda. She tapped the button and saw another bubble:

"You cannot message this person since your privacy settings don't allow it. You need to update your settings to message

ShellPanda."

This all looked like nonsense to Alicia. "Mom?" She looked over the couch into the kitchen "I need help. I don't think I can message Ben in TullyTown."

As Alicia waited for her mom, she saw an avatar running towards hers in TullyTown. It was wearing a red long sleeve shirt with a panda on it. Alicia was pretty sure it was Ben.

"Let's see what we can do." Her mom walked over and looked at the screen. She tapped it a few times and stopped to read something that Alicia was sure her mom wouldn't understand either. Obviously, more nonsense. Her mom tapped the screen again. "Okay, you should be able to message Ben." Her mom squinted at the ID and then looked at Alicia. "I mean, Shell… Panda."

Alicia giggled and her mom just shook her head while smiling. "You'll be able to talk to Ben, but if someone you don't know asks to connect, what should you do?"

"Ask you or Dad," Alicia said.

"Good job." Alicia's mom smiled.

A little bubble popped up on the screen. It was a message from Ben. It read:

ShellPanda: "Welcome to TullyTown! Follow me!"

Alicia started to follow Ben, but his avatar

was moving very fast and Alicia was still new to TullyTown. She soon lost Ben's avatar, but she was pretty sure she knew how to get to the center of town where he was headed.

There were so many different sights to see on her way to the center of town. There were avatars of all colors and shapes, even animals. Some of them were on leashes being walked by avatars and others were wild animals climbing the trees or just sitting on the sidewalks. She still didn't see Ben anywhere, so she tapped on the message button and sent a message to Ben.

aic45901: "I'm in front of the clothing store. Where are you?"

Alicia spun her avatar around looking for Ben. There were a lot of other ones around, but finally she saw the bright red shirt with a panda on it heading towards her. As it got closer, it stopped and jumped up and down. *That was Ben all right.*

ShellPanda: "Follow me. You have to see these sunglasses I found."

He ran into the clothing store and went towards the sunglasses shelf. There he stopped and waited for Alicia.

ShellPanda: "How cool are these!"

On the shelf was a pair of gold-framed sunglasses with sparkling diamonds and black lenses. Alicia thought they would certainly look good on her avatar.

aic45901: "Wow!"

Alicia noticed a number that was in a blue box right above the sunglasses.

aic45901: "What is that number for?"

ShellPanda: "That's how much they cost."

It was a large number.

ShellPanda: "You can work a job, or you can sell things to get credits. You can also ask your parents to buy you credits."

aic45901: "My mom gave me some credits already, but it was only 10."

ShellPanda: "I spent all my credits and the last time I asked my parents for more they told me to go outside and play. I don't ask anymore."

Alicia didn't know how her parents would react to her asking for credits, especially so many for a pair of sunglasses. In fact, she was pretty sure they were not going to give her that much more.

aic45901: "Those glasses are pretty cool, but I don't think my parents will give me the credits. Where can I earn some?"

ShellPanda: "Follow me!"

Ben's avatar ran out of the store and into TullyTown, with Alicia quickly following behind. As she was following Ben, a popup came up on her screen:

"BlueMeg sent you a friend request."

Alicia hovered over the 'Accept' button with her finger while trying to figure out who it might be. She ignored the request since she didn't know who it was, but then she lost Ben again. She saw him stop in front of a large square-shaped store next to a busy street.

ShellPanda: "Here is the pizza shop. You can work here for more credits."

Alicia and Ben's avatars walked into the pizza shop that had red brick walls, a wooden floor, and a huge menu with all the available pizza options above the large ovens.

aic45901: "How do I earn credits?"

ShellPanda: "You wait for orders to come in and then you deliver it somewhere."

aic54901: "That sounds easy."

ShellPanda: "Well, you have fun. I'm going to get in my car and drive around for a bit. I'll see you later."

Ben ran out of the pizza shop. Just as he did, a popup appeared again.

"BlueMeg sent you a friend request."

It seemed like this person BlueMeg really wanted to be friends. Alicia did not know who it could be since the only two people she knew in TullyTown were Ben and Cathy. BlueMeg was neither of them so Alicia decided to ignore the request again and focus instead on delivering pizzas to hungry avatars. She really wanted to earn credits to get those golden sunglasses.

As Alicia's avatar stood in the pizza parlor, she noticed little buttons appearing on the screen with a name and a type of pizza. She tapped one of the buttons and a white pizza box appeared in front of her avatar. She tapped on the pizza box and an arrow appeared at the top of her screen. When she moved around, the arrow pointed in one direction, which she thought meant the direction to take the pizza.

After a few minutes of carrying the pizza, Alicia arrived at a big, neon blue house. Alicia noticed the front door was glowing gold and the arrow was pointing in that direction. As her avatar got closer to the front door, the pizza in her hands disappeared and a number appeared in front of her avatar. The ten credits that she had went up to fifteen.

I need to deliver a lot of pizzas for those sunglasses, she thought. This was very disappointing. She was hoping it wouldn't take too long to earn enough money, but the truth was she was going to have to spend a lot of time in

TullyTown delivering pizzas.

"Is that Tubby Town?" her dad asked as he sat on the couch next to her.

"You mean TullyTown?" Alicia laughed.

"How do you play this game?" he asked.

"It is a game where you can run around a town with other people. You can buy clothes, drive cars, and even work."

Her dad was not that impressed. "I work all day. I don't think I would want to play a game where I work, too."

"Well, there is a really cool pair of sunglasses that I'm trying to earn credits for. Do you want to see them?" Alicia didn't wait for her dad to respond as she moved her little avatar toward the center of town. It wasn't that far from the pizza shop.

"Look out for that tiger!" Her dad pointed to the screen as a tiger was running at full speed in front of Alicia's avatar.

"TullyTown is pretty crazy!" Alicia shrugged since she was feeling like a pro at TullyTown. Her avatar made it to the store and made its way to the sunglasses display. "There they are."

"Those are pretty cool," he said. "What's that number above them?"

"That's the price." Alicia slowly looked up at her dad.

"In real money?" Her dad said with surprise.

"No. You use credits in the game. I can work for them or buy them." Alicia knew her dad was not going to offer any money to purchase more credits.

"Boy, those are expensive, don't you think?"

"Yeah." Alicia looked back at the screen. "But I've only been able to get a few credits from delivering pizzas."

Suddenly a popup came up again: "BlueMeg sent you a friend request."

"Who is BlueMeg?" her dad asked.

"I don't know, but this is the third time they sent me a request. It could be someone I know. I'm not sure though so I did not respond," Alicia said.

"Good thinking. If you don't know them, then I would stay away, too," Dad warned.

"I understand." Alicia looked back at the sunglasses. "Those sure are really cool sunglasses." She smiled to her dad.

"I'm sure I would have to work another job to buy those for you. Good thing you can deliver more pizzas." Her dad kissed her on the top of her head. "It's almost dinner time, so why don't you finish up the game." He got up and walked over to a side table in the living room. "By the way, I set up a little charging area for all our devices. When you are done with your tablet, you can use this to charge it."

He showed her a white cord that worked with her tablet.

Alicia closed the screen and walked over to the table with all of the charging cables on it. She took the one her dad was holding and plugged it into the tablet. She heard the familiar "bloop" sound that meant the tablet was charging.

"Can you come help set the table for dinner, Alicia?" She heard her mom ask from the kitchen.

Alicia ran over to the table and passed out the plates and napkins. As they sat down for dinner, Alicia started to tell her parents all about her adventures in TullyTown.

"...then there was an avatar dressed in a T-Rex costume and he was jumping up and down on a bush!" Alicia said as she scooped some rice on her plate.

"That sounds odd," her mom said and wrinkled up her face. "Did you meet any of your other friends from school in TullyTown?"

"No, just Ben. He showed me around in the game," Alicia said as she took a mouthful of chicken. When she was done chewing, she added, "Although, someone named BlueMeg kept sending me a friend request. I don't know who that is. I only gave my ID to Ben and Cathy."

Her mom looked a little concerned. "Well, it sounds like it's someone you don't need to connect to right now. You can ask your friends tomorrow to see if any of them know who that is or if it is any of them."

Alicia nodded her head and took another bite of dinner.

"Hey, it sounds like TullyTown is a fun and exciting place, but make sure you continue to make good decisions about who you connect with and what you do." Her mom reached over the table and squeezed her hand. "Speaking of good ideas, finish your Brussels sprouts."

Alicia leaned back in her chair and groaned. She was hoping to be able to get through dinner with as few Brussels sprouts as possible.

Once dinner was finished, Alicia helped her parents cleanup the table and then she went to the charging table. Putting her hands on her tablet, she looked at her dad. "Just for a few minutes before bedtime, please?" Her dad was washing some of the dishes but he agreed she could have a little more time.

Alicia smiled and picked up the tablet from the charging table. She tapped on the TullyTown icon and waited for it to load. Just as she saw her avatar in TullyTown, another invite from BlueMeg appeared on the screen. Once more, she let the invite bubble disappear and instead went back to delivering more pizzas. She was earning credits, but she was far away from the credits she needed for those spiffy sunglasses.

Soon her eyes were getting heavy and she heard her dad asking her to get ready for bed. Alicia put the tablet back on the charging table and took a quick shower. After she got her pajamas on and said goodnight to her parents, she laid in bed drifting off to sleep as she thought of all the things she did in TullyTown that evening. More importantly, she was curious about BlueMeg. *Who was it?*

CHAPTER 7

There was a knock at Alicia's bedroom door as she slowly opened her eyes. "Rise and shine, sleepy head," her dad called into her room to wake her.

Alicia rolled out of bed and started her routine to get ready for school. As she passed by her calendar on the way to the bathroom, she saw it was library day. She brightened up a little when she saw that since library day was one of her favorite days in school. Other than science class, where there was always the possibility of something exploding, going to the library was the highlight of her week. She liked getting out of the classroom for a little and being able to look for some new books.

She quickly got dressed for school and then ran to the kitchen, grabbed a bowl and spoon, and poured herself some cereal. As she stuffed her mouth with the fruity balls of cereal, her mom leaned her head out of the bedroom door. "Only a few more minutes until the bus is here, so you better get your stuff together."

Alicia ate the rest of her cereal like she was never going to eat again. She hopped up from the table and quickly put on her jacket and grabbed her school bag. Then she ran out the door as she heard the squeaking of the bus tires.

Cathy was already at the bus stop as Alicia ran up. "One of these days you'll get to the bus stop early." Cathy smiled.

The two girls climbed onto the bus and took their normal seats. Alicia began to tell Cathy some of the things she saw in TullyTown and Cathy told her some of the videos she watched on VideoMe.

"TullyTown would be so much better if you accepted *my* friend request."

Alicia looked across the aisle at Megan who was sitting with her arms crossed and a hurt look on her face.

"Oh, I didn't know you had my ID," Alicia said.

"I heard you talking to Cathy and Ben yesterday. Ben put the paper down that you gave him and I saw it. I wrote down your ID so I could send you a request," Megan said.

Alicia thought for a few seconds. "Are you BlueMeg?"

Megan sat up in her seat. "Yes!"

"Oh. I would have given you my ID, but you weren't there when I gave it to Cathy and Ben." Alicia knew Megan was a little hurt, but she was also concerned that Megan got her ID without asking. Alicia would have eventually given it to Megan, at least she thought she would have.

"Well, now you know who I am. I have a big house in TullyTown that I wanted to show you. It has a two-car garage, four bedrooms, and six bathrooms," Megan boasted.

"That's a lot of bathrooms." Cathy was wondering what anyone would do with that many bathrooms.

"A house?" Alicia asked.

"Yeah, you can build one or buy one. A lot of times it's easier to just build one," Megan said.

"I haven't gotten that far yet. I just started playing. But I saw these cool sunglasses I want to get!"

"Well, my mom and dad gave me some money over Christmas that I used to get credits. I was able to build a big house." As Megan said this, she stretched out her arms to show the size of her house. Megan smiled and said, "Also, the walls are bright purple."

"Oh, I'd like to see that," Alicia said as the bus pulled up to the school.

As Alicia walked into her classroom, she saw Ben who looked down as he saw her. "I had another close call with a fence in my car last night. And maybe some squirrels."

"I think you need driving lessons." Alicia laughed and shook her head at the thought of Ben crashing his car. But there was no time to think about scared squirrels and Ben's terrible driving. Alicia's teacher was lining up the class for library, which was an even more special day today because Alicia heard that the librarian was showing the class some of the new devices the school just purchased.

Alicia raced to the front of the line and waited patiently for everyone else to line up and quiet down. Once the teacher had everyone's attention, she started to move the line down the hallway. They only had to stop a few times so her teacher could ask the class to keep the noise down and stay in line. They finally reached the library and the class took their seats at the tables spread out around the room.

Mr. Mitchell was standing at the front of the library waiting for all the students to settle in their seats. He soon began. "Today we have some new selections in the fiction category that you will want to take a look at on the table in the back." The librarian pointed towards the back of the room full of books. "Everyone remembers what fiction means, right?"

One of the boys in the class yelled out, "It means fake!"

"That's right, fiction means the books are not written about real events. There are also new non-fiction books about famous people in history that are on the table next to the fiction books."

Mr. Mitchell then walked over to the desk near the front of the library and picked up something that looked a bit like a thin book. "Who knows what this is?" he asked as he raised the object above his head for all the class to see. Almost everyone raised their hand. The librarian pointed to one of the boys sitting in the front row. "Michael, what is this?"

"A tablet?" the boy sounded slightly unsure

of himself.

"Sure is," Mr. Mitchell said. "Now, the rest of our time here in the library today we are going to review how to use the tablet. It will help you find books here in the library and you will also learn how to get some books ordered for home. Later in the month we will learn to do research on topics that you are interested in."

Alicia was pretty excited to use her newfound tablet skills at the library.

"There are not enough for everyone, but there is one on each table. So I want you to work as groups at each table and I want one person from your table to lead while I show the class how we are going to use it here," he continued.

Alicia looked around the table she was sitting at and saw Megan across from her who immediately reached for the tablet at the center of the table. The two other boys at the table moved their chairs closer to Megan so they could see the screen. Megan was soon swiping and dragging her fingers across the screen.

"All eyes forward so I can show you how to use the tablet," Mr. Mitchell said to the class as he noticed almost all of the students were focused on the tablet at their table.

Everyone at Alicia's table looked up—except Megan. She was still focused on the tablet, obviously trying to do something, but Alicia wasn't sure what she was doing.

"All right, everyone let's go through some of the things you can do. First...."

Alicia looked back at Megan who was still playing with the screen as the librarian was giving instructions. "He is trying to tell us how to use that thing," Alicia whispered to Megan.

"I know what I'm doing with it," Megan whispered back. "I posted a picture this morning on SocialBee. I want to see it."

"Megan and Alicia? Are you two paying attention?" The entire class looked back at Alicia's table. Megan put the tablet down on the table and both she and Alicia responded, "Yes."

Mr. Mitchell was clearly not happy about the disruption, but he soon started again by holding up his tablet to show the class the screen. "At the top of the library app you will see our school name. That's how you know you are in the right place. Touch the 'New Books' button." The librarian touched the button and the screen changed. "This will show you the new books the library received this month." He walked over to Alicia's table and looked down at the tablet. "Right here." He pointed to the icon on the top of the screen.

Megan picked the tablet up again and tapped on "New Books". The screen changed to show a menu of book covers and a description of each book. Alicia saw a few that looked interesting so she moved closer to see the screen. However, as the librarian walked away, Megan opened another screen on the tablet. Alicia didn't recognize what was on the screen, but at the top in large letters was "SocialBee."

"Megan, you are going to get us in trouble!" Alicia said quietly.

Megan started to swipe up on the screen and Alicia saw a screen full of pictures and other little icons. Then Megan stopped on a picture of a clearly upset cat wearing an ugly sweater. "Hmph… only seven more likes since this morning," Megan said with frustration as she stared at the screen.

Alicia looked at the tablet where she saw a picture of Megan's cat, Lester. He was in Megan's bedroom sitting on the bed with a very unhappy look on his face. Alicia was pretty sure it had to do with the bright yellow sweater he was wearing. On the wall of Megan's room were some posters, pictures of her family, and a banner from their school. There were some dirty clothes on the floor, and some homework on Megan's desk next to a stack of books.

"It took me a long time to catch Lester and dress him. I thought I would get more likes." Megan whispered, but was still clearly upset.

Alicia wasn't sure what it meant to get a "like" but it sounded like it was important to Megan. "Do you get something for a 'like'?"

Megan made a face similar to Lester's in the picture. "Yes. I feel happy when someone likes something I did, especially when I put in a lot of work to do it."

Megan and Alicia didn't notice the librarian had made his way back to their table. "Megan, what are you doing?" He stepped closer to the table and looked down at the tablet.

"I was just looking for something," Megan lied.

The librarian didn't say anything as he looked back down at Megan and picked up the tablet. "Megan, please follow me." Megan hung her head low and slowly got up from her seat.

Alicia couldn't remember the last time she saw someone get in this kind of trouble in class. She wasn't sure where Mr. Mitchell was going to take Megan, but Alicia could only assume it was to the principal's office. Alicia didn't know anyone personally who had ever been to the principal's office.

The librarian tapped on a few things on the tablet and then handed it back to Alicia. He looked back up to the rest of the class. "Under each book on the screen, it will tell you where in the library it's located. I want you to spend some time looking through the new books section and locate some books you want to check out of the library. When I get back, I will answer any questions you have." He walked Megan out into the hallway.

The other boys at the table pulled their chairs closer to Alicia. The screen was back to the page with the new books. However, as Alicia was looking at the screen all she could think about was Megan and how much trouble she was in.

After library was over, Alicia and her class went back to their classroom, but there was still no sign of Megan. Alicia's teacher asked the class to take their seats and get out their vocabulary books.

As Alicia pulled her book out, she looked out of the classroom window and saw Megan getting in a car with her mom. Her mom looked very upset. *This was not going to be good for Megan*, Alicia thought. Alicia turned back to the front of the class where her teacher was already starting the lesson.

As the day continued, Alicia felt more worried about Megan. But it was soon time to get on the afternoon bus home. Alicia walked over to Cathy while she was packing her bag to leave.

"Did you hear about Megan?" Cathy asked when she saw Alicia.

Alicia just nodded sadly and was soon joined by Ben who was dragging his feet a bit. "I heard Megan went home with her mom after she got sent to the principal's office."

All three of them looked down at their feet as they began to think about what that meant for Megan. Alicia felt especially bad since she tried to tell Megan to pay attention and she thought she should have done a little more to keep her out of trouble.

"She was looking to see how many 'likes' she had on a picture," Alicia stated.

"Was that the one with Lester in it? Lester did not look like he was having a good time." Ben looked like he was about to smile but then remembered how much trouble Megan was in.

Alicia let out a sigh. She was pretty sure getting sent home from school was not worth a picture of a grumpy cat in a sweater.

"I've never been sent to the principal's office." Ben looked like he was thinking very hard. "And I don't ever want to be sent to the principal's office." They each grabbed their bags and walked to the bus line after hearing their bus number being called over the speakers.

Taking their seats for the ride home, they started to forget about what happened to Megan as the normal buzz on the bus soon took over and they began talking about their day. Before long, they were laughing about a silly song they heard a group of kids singing at lunch. They each were trying to remember the words of the song, and after some help from a few other kids on the bus, they were all singing the song most of the ride home. The bus driver even joined in after a while.

CHAPTER 8

When Alicia arrived home from school that day, she put her bag down and saw her mom in the living room. Sitting down next to her, Alicia began to explain to her mom what happened to Megan that day in the library. Alicia really felt like she could have done more to help Megan.

"Sounds like Megan is going to be in a lot of trouble," Alicia's mom said. "Those tablets belong to the school and should not be used for other things. While it's okay to be upset that Megan got in trouble, this was not your fault."

Alicia picked up her school bag and made her way to her bedroom to spend some time on homework. She tried to concentrate, but it was difficult while she was still wondering how Megan was doing. After she was able to focus long enough to complete her homework, she closed her books and organized her papers before putting everything in her schoolbag for the next day.

She walked to the kitchen to grab a snack since her dad was starting to cook dinner. "Can I go on my tablet for a bit while you make dinner?" Alicia asked her dad.

"Are you finished with your homework?"

"Yes, I did it as soon as I came home from school."

"Sure thing then," he said as he tasted the sauce he was making. When he started to cough and make a sour face, Alicia knew something was not right. "Oh boy, that needs some fixing."

Alicia shook her head with a smile. Her dad's recipes were sometimes great and other times experimental. Leaving the kitchen, Alicia picked up her tablet from the table and sat on the couch. *Tablet in one hand, apple in the other.*

Even though she was still working on earning some credit in TullyTown, the amount of credits she needed to buy those crazy sunglasses seemed impossible. She remembered Megan talked about building a house and getting accessories for it. Alicia thought that was a better use of her time. At least she would get something out of it soon rather than working for what seemed like forever to get a pair of digital sunglasses.

She went to a part of TullyTown where she would be able to build a house. She found an empty space and a "Build" button appeared on the screen. She tapped the button and a few outlines of a house appeared in a menu on the screen. She picked out one that looked like a good start for the house she wanted. The outline of the house she picked floated above her avatar. She was able to move it around the screen and eventually put it on an open area in TullyTown. With this, she saw a few of her credits disappear.

Alicia walked her avatar around the house. It was large and very empty. The "Build" button was still on the screen, so she tapped on it again. This time she had a menu of different items like windows, doors, furniture, and other things for a house. She started to put in the walls, windows, doors, and steps all around the house. Not everything made sense in its location, but nobody was really going to live in the house. *Fake houses could look any way you want them to*, she thought to herself.

While placing things around the house, she watched her hard-earned credits slowly disappear. What is more, a lot of other building items were added to the list but they became gray, which meant she would need more credits to get them. With what credits she had left, she decided to put in furniture for her living room and bedroom. With a few taps of the screen, she had a bed for herself and a cat bed next to it. Alicia was pretty sure she was going to eventually get a cat for the house. In the living room, she only had enough credits to buy a small chair and put down a rug. The rug had a very crazy zigzag pattern in purple and gold. It was bright, silly, and perfect for her new house.

Alicia's dad walked in and sat down next to her on the couch. He looked at her screen and yelled, "Yikes! What's the deal with that rug!" Alicia and her dad began to laugh.

Alicia's avatar took a few trips around her new house showing her dad all the different things she put in it throughout all of the rooms, including the floors. She was happy with what she built, but, more importantly, she was out of credits.

"I like what you made, but why don't you take a break for the evening and get ready for dinner?"

"Ok, Dad."

Alicia's dad walked back into the kitchen. Alicia walked towards the charging table to charge her tablet again before dinner. First though, she wanted to look at the picture Megan put on SocialBee. She went into the kitchen to ask her dad to help her find Megan in the app. After a bit of searching, her dad found Megan's profile and handed the tablet back to Alicia.

"Remember, dinner is almost ready. You have just a few minutes."

Alicia scrolled through the pictures and messages. Megan was very active on SocialBee and had pictures of her cat, vacations and places she went, her house and room, and lots of different pictures of food. It seemed that wherever she had her tablet, she would post pictures. Alicia saw an option on the screen to send a friend request to Megan. She found it odd that she was able to see all of Megan's stuff even though they were not friends in the app. She tapped the button to send a request to Megan.

Looking at Megan's profile, Alicia started to think about what happened in the library and wondered how Megan was doing. As Alicia scrolled through the pictures Megan posted, she found the picture of Megan's cat

in the sweater. Alicia tapped the "like" button.
She hoped when Megan saw it, she would feel
like someone appreciated her effort with
Lester.

Alicia heard her dad call for dinner, so she
put the tablet on the charging table, and
joined her parents at the dinner table. As
Alicia and her parents sat for dinner, they
talked about what happened at the library.
Alicia felt a little better after talking to her
parents and as she fell asleep that night, she
wondered whether she would see Megan the
next day at school.

***

The bus ride the next day was much like
many others. Alicia was describing the dinner
her dad made the night before to Cathy. "It
wasn't the worse thing I've tasted, but a pizza
would have been a better option. But I guess
pizza is always a better option." Alicia laughed
as the bus slowed to a stop in front of
Megan's house.

Alicia and Cathy peered over their seat to
see Megan walking slowly down the aisle.
Megan took her seat across the aisle and
looked out the window.

"Hey, Megan. How are you doing?" Alicia

knew Megan could not have been doing too well.

"Okay, I guess," Megan said without looking over.

"What happened at the principal's office?" Cathy leaned past Alicia as she asked. She was very curious since she never talked to anyone who was sent to the principal's office.

Megan told Alicia and Cathy, and everyone else who was sitting nearby, that the principal had called her parents and told them she was misusing school property. Normally, the school would have made her stay home from school for three days, but because this was the first time she had been to the principal's office and she was normally a good student, the principal decided to give her a warning and send her home for the day. Staying home for three days might sound like fun, but not when it was a punishment. Megan's parents were especially unhappy and being sent home was the least of her concerns.

"I got grounded," Megan said as she slumped in her seat a bit. "No tablet for two whole weeks."

Some of the kids listening began to look at others with a nervous look on their faces. Alicia felt bad for Megan and felt even worse when she saw how upset Megan looked.

"That sounds pretty rough, Megan," Cathy said.

Alicia leaned over and whispered in Cathy's ear. Both girls smiled and nodded.

"What if we gave up our tablets for two weeks with you?" Alicia offered.

Megan looked over at the two girls and started to smile. "You don't have to do that for me. It is my fault that I got grounded."

"It's okay, Megan. I think it would be good to take a break for a bit. I don't mind," Alicia said.

"Me neither," Cathy agreed.

Megan's smile got bigger.

"I'll join you, too," Ben spoke up as he peered over the back of the seat. "Besides, I think the squirrels of TullyTown need a break from my driving."

They all began to laugh.

ASK ALICIA

Throughout the book Alicia and her friends faced many challenges to using technology safely and securely. To learn more about why these issues could be a security or privacy concern as well as best practices to stay safe while using technology, follow "Alicia Connected" on Facebook or at:

BOOK TWO OF ALICIA CONNECTED

Coming in Summer of 2021!

Halloween is here, and it is Alicia's favorite time of year. What's not to like about dressing up in a costume and getting free candy? But there is something even more exciting happening this year. For the first time, Alicia and her friends are throwing a virtual party in TullyTown!

Putting together a party in TullyTown isn't easy, and Alicia and her friends want to do the best they can to make sure it is enjoyed by plenty of avatars in TullyTown. For one of Alicia's friends, getting ready to throw a TullyTown party leads to looking for easy treats. But what if it's a trick?

ABOUT THE AUTHOR

Derek Fisher has been in the engineering field for several decades. He has extensive experience designing systems in both hardware and software at companies large and small. He became interested in security and pursued a graduate degree in cybersecurity from Boston University as well as obtained several security certifications. He continues to work professionally as an architect, leader, university instructor, and evangelist in the security space. He is a frequent speaker at industry conferences where he provides his security insight to multiple fields and disciplines.

Derek started Securely Built with the intention of bringing security awareness to a larger audience including educators, parents, children, and technical professionals. He is a loving father and husband which has provided him the inspiration to write this book.

You can find out more about Derek and his background at www.securelybuilt.com

Made in the USA
Monee, IL
30 August 2022

12932802R00052